PRAISE

"*You Go Home* is filled with sharp turns, stop signs, highway berms, traffic circles, and porta-potties. These stories haunt and prod and poke and hide and rejoice and mourn and burrow their way into your daily thoughts until you're a tiny version of yourself in some stranger's home, staged in their expansive railroad diorama, legs crossed, reading this chapbook. Steven Sherrill is a trickster and a haunter and a maker-upper of words and worlds. Latch yourself onto his wagon, follow him home."

 —**Sherrie Flick,** author of *I Have Not Considered Consequences* and *Whiskey, Etc.*

"The stared and steeped funicular fictions of Steven Sherrill's *You Go Home* call to mind Pittsburgh's famous Incline Elevators—reticulated, cantilevered, cubistic, cabled cabs of gravity declining machines clanking askance with uncanny steam punkery. They do transport you, these cock-eyed shocks, to another clime and climb, while at the same time providing some stunning sites to be seen—defamiliarized, deformed, dimensionless. Timeless and out of time, all aboard these fine sublime clap trapped contraptions of wonder."

 —**Michael Martone,** author of *Table Talk & Second Thoughts* and *Plain Air: Sketches from Winesburg, Indiana*

"*You Go Home* by Steven Sherrill is a magical chapbook filled with whimsy that sneaks up on you and grips your heart and your ear and won't let go until all of its secrets are whispered. Sherrill writes with the language of a poet, but with the surprise of a stand-up comic. He threads moods and tones full of surprises with characters who won't let you forget them. Raising a ruckus, living inside of pockets, and hungering for the lost days of youth. Readers, you won't regret your time with these peculiar and stunning stories. "

 —**Tommy Dean,** author of *Hollows* and Editor of *Fractured Lit*

YOU GO HOME

STEVEN SHERRILL

YOU GO HOME

Edited by Tommy Dean.

Cover design by Emelie Mano.

Interior design by Julianne Johnson.

Red Mare Press / Discover New Art, LLC

70 SW Century Drive, Suite 100442, Bend, Oregon 97702

www.redmarepress.com

Red Mare Press is a division of Discover New Art, LLC.

The Red Mare Press name and logo are trademarks of Discover New Art, LLC.

The publisher is not responsible for websites (or their content) that are not owned by the publisher.

ISBN 979-8-9901838-6-5

Printed in the United States of America.

For my family. All of them.

CONTENTS

THERE IS A PLAUSIBLE EXPLANATION FOR WHY THE BRILLIANT, THOUGH FURTIVE, APIARIST WAS FOUND BURIED BENEATH AN AVALANCHE OF ANTIQUE WOODEN CRUTCHES, MILDEWED CRUTCHES OF EVERY IMAGINABLE SIZE, SAID TO HAVE COME FROM THE BASEMENT OF THE

ACKNOWLEDGEMENTS

INTRODUCTION

There's something magical about a flash fiction chapbook. Both forms were meant for each other. A sharp cut of narrative, a quick breath or a gasp, a dip into luxurious storytelling. The chapbook, though it often hides on a bookshelf, is the perfect tag along for a short trip to the park or a long flight. Like a notebook, it's a steady companion, waiting for you to crack its spine, light your eyes upon its pages, and allow yourself a few minutes of wonder.

Speaking of wonder, I'm so excited to get this book into the hands of readers. Steven Sherrill writes with abandon, with vulnerability and honesty, and a mash-up of whimsy and ribald comedy that often takes readers by surprise. Sherrill has had a long career of creativity, from writing to music, to art. Just look again at this cover! It's pure Steven Sherrill and it's gorgeous.

Welcome to the world of the men and women of Sherrill's imagination. Realism, but with a yank and a twist toward the comedic, but with whit and soul, and all the right pieces subtlety arranged for our enjoyment.

Dear reader, I imagine you sitting down by a lake, the soft buzz of insects at your side while you hold on to this special book, while you reimagine your own lives, while you wonder at the lives of these heartbreaking and beguiling men, women, and children who are all trying to make it in an off-kilter and Picasso-esque world that may not quite look like ours, but the feelings are true and vulnerable, and finally valuable for they take us outside of ourselves for just a minute, and we can relax, because Sherrill knows how to tell a story.

—Tommy Dean

MY BROTHER, NAMED AND UNNAMED

My brother is the smallest man in the world.

I'm not even kidding. Most of the time, he lives in my jacket pocket. One kernel of popcorn will keep him going for weeks. It's hot in there, in my jacket pocket, and hard to breathe, probably. But he needs so little air. Sometimes, I take him out to impress a girl. It rarely works. When we drive, well, when I drive, I keep him tucked behind one of the plastic air conditioner vents. If he complains too much, I just turn the fan up a notch. And, I'll confess this only to you: on more than one occasion, I've used him to get out of a speeding ticket. My brother used to ride on the rearview mirror, laughing and swaying to beat the band. But once, he fell into my iced latte. Talked nonstop for three days. Annoying as hell. Don't tell him this, but I thought he was going to drown, there in my coffee. I thought he was a goner. I got really scared. That's when I started planning his funeral. Don't tell him this, either. I've been adding details ever since. The service. The guest list. Eulogists out the wazoo. More hibiscus than you can shake a stick at. Violinists to boot. And good god, the foodstuffs. Don't tell him. You can come. I'll put you on the invite list. It's going to blow your mind. It'll be the biggest funeral in the world.

My brother is a tree stump.

Don't laugh. He's sensitive about it. My brother is a tree stump. Ash, maybe. Or poplar. I don't pay that much attention sometimes. Axe-bitten, either way. Speaking of which, I propped a piece of plywood against him, painted a bullseye on it. "Stop it," he said. Then tripped me with a dead root. He used to make fun of my skinny legs. Our mother never knew what got carved into the bark of his trunk. He's always after me about

the goddamn chipmunks. They won't leave him alone. But I'm busy, so. When I want him to shut up, I whisper *polesaw* and *gaff*. We both fear the word *arborist*. But not for the same reasons. He did, once, in deep winter, reveal that he wished he was a pine. A pitch pine. Pinus rigida. Though, maybe he said walnut. I don't pay that much attention. The best times? After the sun gets low, and there's no need for shade. I lean against him, that stump of him, and we share a beer. We look up and up together and talk about all of his branches.

My brother speaks red dirt. Only.

No. Turpentine too, but not so fluently. And only in the hottest part of July. One time, he tried to speak to us in drafting pencil and ruler. He got choked on eraser crumbs, and we almost lost him. The esophagus is wily and cannot be trusted. One time, in a cave made of packed red clay, he pretended to speak Marine. Ready to die for our country. We almost lost him. If not for the flounder bone caught in our throats, collectively, we would have wailed. That time he joined the choir? Every note, a glazed pot. A cracked vessel. If not for the throats caught in our bones, we would have wept. The mouth is an exit wound. Everything from this point forward will be a lie.

LET'S SAY, TRIPTYCH

LET'S SAY YOU FOLLOW HER HOME. The barefoot girl on the corner of Union Avenue, near where Nut Creek gnaws at the back steps of a couple churches and the financially struggling crisis center. She cuts her own hair, with garden clippers. Let's say. Hacks. The look on her face, maybe suffering, maybe bliss. You can't decide. Can't tell. Let's say she's talking to herself. Or singing. In this version, you don't know the words. "Stop," you say. "Don't," you say. "Let me teach you." Let's say you follow her home. Let's say you don't go to your roomful of undergrads, ready or not, for your Ekphrastic Writing exercise. You follow her home. Except it's not home, and you just want to wash her feet. "I know things about art," you say. "I want to teach you," you say. She recoils. "You're nobody's savior," she says, then disembowels you with her shears.

No. No. No. What happens is this. Let's say you follow her. Home. The girl on the corner with the hair and the rage. Your real wife, your real kids. Too bad. You have to be true. To your dream. You stop teaching. Devote your life to her feet. Carvings of same, perfectly rendered, in miniature, in soap. Try not to think about her hair. You offer her endless skulls of roadkill deer. Only. You offer her viable sperm. "I know things about art," you say. "I want to teach you," you say. She recoils. "This is ridiculous," she says. "I'm not your savior." She takes the clippers, having hidden them, for all these years, in her mouth. Or maybe it was her sock drawer. Either way, she takes the clippers. Disembowels you.

Hey. Come on, now. Let's say the truth. Let's say the truth is you are a coward. But no more or less than anybody else. Let's say you go home. Real home. Enough so, anyway. Your wife is mad at you. There's a tomato sauce stain on her shirt, disappearing into the pocket over her heart. You sob, but only inside. You were supposed to help your daughter with her homework. Social Studies. You're mad at all of them, but you can't remember why. Let's say you want to tell her about something you saw. Out there. Let's say you can only gesture. Let's say she sees it, that gesture, and knows enough, and in her knowing, reaches, returning her own. Gesture. Lord help us, the depth of that love disembowels you.

HONEYMOON UNDERWEAR

HE LOVES GOING INTO A LINGERIE STORE for the first time. Loves it. Loves how the salesclerks size him up. Their unspoken negotiations over who'd approach him. Business trips, different cities, new neighborhoods. Once or twice in his life, a foreign country. Stores named Hanky-Panky, or j'Adore. Stores with Touch or Venus or Silk in the name. Doesn't matter.

He loves catching the salesclerk's eye, *his* salesclerk's eye, as she walks toward him. His age, maybe. Even older. Sometimes much younger. Doesn't matter. She walks through the mannequin's hush-hush wantonness. Smiling.

Sometimes, in posh little blocks, maybe tucked between a bakery specializing in French macarons and a shoe store with boots of the most exotic leathers. But just as often, on less than chichi streets. A liquor store on one corner, a struggling deli at the other. Doesn't matter. He loves it every time.

They come to him. Younger. Older. Smiling. Ready. Willing to help. They know, they can tell, just by how he comports himself, not to offer anything bright red, anything crotchless. They weave him through the displays, some armless, legless, some headless, each and every one no less desirable for the lacks. Back to the deepest, sweetest part of the store. Where the light is just right, and the mirrors play the best tricks. Where they—the salesclerks, the women, the girls—do not pry, they merely, expertly, lead. *Business. I'm in business.* He practices saying it, though it's been true for years. They listen. They see him. They allow things. Looking the other way, or smiling *that* smile, when he reaches to touch a fabric, a lace trim. He likes a bustier like just so. He wants this cut, this lay over the hips. These soft colors. They nod and *mmm* approvingly.

Those women, the older ones with the beautiful full bellies, fuller breasts, shorter decisive hair, the younger ones, the girls, sometimes diminutive, birdlike, sometimes all legs and arms, their breasts and behinds locked in and unwavering, and with any one of them he can tell when they're getting close to that magical moment, that delicious instant when she, his salesclerk, asks a version of this. *What size are we looking for today?*

Everything stops. He looks right at her. Doesn't matter. She offers herself. Front, back, sides. He holds his hands up cupping imaginary breasts. *She's about your size,* he says. Doesn't matter. Looks at her. Palms imaginary buttocks. *She's about your size,* he says. Together they suss out his need. Select the perfect set, with the perfect fit. *Would you like this gift wrapped?* they ask. Always. *Yes,* he says. *Please,* he says. Always.

Back home, days, sometimes weeks, later, he cleans the grime of travel away as best he can. He puts on his good shirt. Sometimes, even, a tie. Combs his thinning hair. Takes the #11 bus. Takes his gift-wrapped box. There's a stop less than a block away from Keystone Care. His wife lies on the third floor. The window faces east. A Kmart. Twenty years into multiple sclerosis, and she doesn't move, doesn't see, doesn't speak anymore. The nurses leave them alone. He takes a cool sponge, a damp sponge, strokes her lips, her face. *There's my beautiful girl,* he says. *I got you something special,* he says. She used to call it honeymoon underwear. Racing panties. *So sexy, I don't know if I can control myself,* he says. Every time. He takes the gift-wrapped box, opens the closet door, puts it inside with so very many other gift-wrapped boxes.

NO, MISTER DEATH!

SEE ME THERE, THE BOY in the Polaroid. The boy in the Superman pajamas, with the red cape. See. Watch me ball my little fists and puff up my little boy chest. See me rise out of that picture, raise my head, and speak. *No, Mister Death!* I say. *You cannot have my papa today,* I say. *Go away!* And he does. Mister Death reels against the blow of my ferocity, writhes, shrivels into a tiny speck of dust and drifts into a beam of pure sunlight that angles in from the only window visible in the picture, through which my father can be seen mowing the yard. Poof, Mister Death is gone. Doesn't show his face for seventy-three years. Seventy-three years later, I tuck the funeral card into a clear sleeve on the last page of the photo album and close it just as my son comes into the room. *What're you doing, Pop?* he asks. *Just thinking,* I say, and reach up to straighten his little boy tie. *What are you thinking about?* he asks, with an emphasis on *about*. A beam of pure sunlight divides the space between us. I look over his young shoulder, through the window, and hopefully. *Superman,* I say. *Who's Superman?* my son asks. Kids these days, I think. *You are,* I say. *You are.*

EFFIGY

IT WAS A PRETTY GOOD IDEA, putting effigies of himself all around town. He remembers getting it, the idea, during an election year. A rowdy mob crowding around an effigy of some politician. Maybe cheering. Maybe about to burn it. Either way, he liked the energy.

The first few, while recognizable, weren't so convincing. Lopsided, lumpy. Questionable complexions. Dressed wrong. And haphazardly distributed. It was not uncommon to see an early effigy, in a misshapen lump, out behind the Dollar Store. But he got better and better with the plaster heads. With the flesh-colored paint. The hair. After depleting his own closet for clothes that fit right, he became a savvy Goodwill shopper.

Soon enough, he wised up to the importance of placement. Location location location. Initially, the effigies were deployed in *his* best interest. In the sheltered bus stop, out of the rain. At the little desk in the basement of the library, where he filled interlibrary loan orders. At the DMV. At the dentist's office. Early in lines for movie tickets, flu shots, the new iPhone. But before long, altruism reared its ugly head.

He wanted to do some good. He started placing effigies with an eye toward civic duty. He took two seats at the public radio telethon phonebank. He kept a steady eye on the bins at the recycling center—this color glass goes here, and that plastic goes there. He was a regular in the gazebo at the retirement village. And he was always found giving out **I Voted** stickers at the polling place.

It was exhausting work. Work that took over his house. Everything was covered in plaster dust and paint. He considered hiring an apprentice or taking on an intern. But decided against both. Hard hard work, but so very worth it. Sure enough, people started to talk. To take notice. Rumors flew hither and yon. *Have you seen that guy? Who is that guy? I heard he saved a kid from drowning, caught a baby falling out of a window, prevented a false arrest, bought groceries for the poor*—and on and on until—*let's get his input about this plan, make sure he supports that idea, I hope he runs for school board. For sheriff. For mayor.*

Early one morning, years into the project, with no end in sight, there came a faint knock at his back door. Papery, weak. He rubbed his weary eyes. Got up from the pallet, where he'd taken to sleeping, on the kitchen floor. Took a steadying breath and opened up. There they stood. All of them. The sun caught in the dew on their plaster heads. The yard was full. Spilling over into the neighbor's yards. *We're hungry,* they said, then again. *We're hungry.* He looked at them. All. He could see it was true. Overwhelmed, he wanted to sob, but there wasn't time. He opened the door wide. *Come in, fellas, come in, and make yourselves at home. Let's get you something good to eat.*

ALTAR CALL

When Reverend Smawley plucked his right eyeball out—the plastic one—to hold over the congregation, the church-honeys swooned. Half the backsliders, pursed-lipped and guilt-washed, sat like they just eked out a pew-poot. The others, whooping like no tomorrow. From the edge of the sagging stage, I heard everything clear as a bell. The tent went quiet. True reverence. Anticipation. Then, a soft-wet thwack as the eyeball left the socket; that was all she wrote. Oh the weeping and wailing.

Besides folding chairs and passing collection plates, I drove, and played the organ. But—self-taught—by that time in the sermon, all I could do was barely keep up. My fingers, useless little sinners. Smawley stomping, hollering how "Jesus come down, as a piece of bailing wire! Took my eye!" When medical science filled up the hole with a worthless bauble, Jesus came back. Blessed him with *special* sight. "Come on!" he said. Commanded. "Come look in this hole! See for yourself!"

Every night, his good eye patched, his worldly vision snuffed out, he gave the call. Sinners spilled into the aisles, ready for miracles. Small or large. Grocery lists, government cards, testimonials and prayer requests, offered up to that empty socket. Smawley read them all. "Go home," he'd say. "Take them little red panties off and burn them. B'leve on the Lord." "Go home," he'd say. "Turn away from that liquor bottle, them pills. Turn away from this vile and wicked earth," he'd say. "Towards Calvary."

I looked into that hole one time. We'd stopped for gas. I came out with two cans of beer. A bag of pork rinds. Set them on the roof of the Plymouth while I pumped. The reverend, wore slap out from doing the Lord's work, clutching his thick, greasy bible—greasy from the Lord's work—slept. Head laid against the Plymouth's rolled up window.

The black patch, in sleep, had slipped down the holy man's cheek. The plastic bauble, the unblinking profane whole of it, tucked away in a pocket somewhere. What remained—the absence—the empty eye, gaped heavenward. I knelt on the oil-stained pavement. I pressed my nose to the glass. I looked into that hole. I seen it all. You better believe it.

AIR SHOW

"**Look up, honey,**" **he said.** "I can't see, Papa," she said. "There," he said, and pointed the way. It was his weekend. A long one, with the holiday. Long. Solo parenting. He was new at this business. Determined to do right. Paid extra for those bleacher seats. Hours of bleacher seats. Looked up all the livelong day. Watched the summer sky shot through and through.

Everybody thought the black biplane with the checkered stripe was going to hit the ground. Its three-cylinder engine spit and sputtered to a stop in the cloudless blue, then, nose aimed at the earth, fell and fell and fell. His daughter leaned in, took his arm. Trembled. Her tiny heart ready. To bear witness. *Not bad,* he thought. He felt pretty good. About things. About himself, even, there on the hard plank seat. He tried to think of anybody he knew that was a better father. Tried.

At the last instant, in the nick of time, just under the wire, not a minute to spare, the biplane's engine caught, roared to life. Streams of red, white, and blue smoke spiraled from its tail and wingtips as the plane swooped low over the crowd, rocking its wings. Air show. Waving and waving. His daughter waved back.

"Nonnie says you have too many hobbies," she said. He knew what Nonnie meant by that. He checked his wallet. Couldn't afford the helicopter ride. But they had corn dogs and French fries and caramel apples and had their picture taken in the cockpit of an honest-to-god fighter jet. In the open hangar, they petted some greyhounds from the rescue. Saw somebody giving autographs.

When the F-22, the Raptor, fired its pair of thrust vectoring jets, it was like the whole world melted. Sight and sound. His daughter nuzzled into his shoulder. Whimpered, but just a little. "Look up, honey," he said.

"This is important stuff," he said. When the pilot kicked the nose vertical and stabbed the sky, straight up and out of sight, it was almost…it was just…. "Did you ever see anything so…" somebody said. "I never felt anything so…" somebody said. Behind him, somebody said, "America." And another, "We can do anything."

Anything. He looked around. It was his weekend. His air show. The helicopter, with its solipsistic bug-eye, skirted the perimeter, settled in a dusty patch of grass near the Porta-Johns. The most wholesome family he'd ever seen piled out, oo-ing and ahh-ing. He looked at his daughter. He pulled out his wallet. He dug deep.

Later, lying in their shared Motel 6 bed, the ceiling fan chopped the humid night air into manageable bits. Ears full of jet roar, still. Everything on fire. On fire. So very much sun. He felt good. Different, somehow. He couldn't put a name on it, though. Then his daughter spoke up. "Papa," she said. "My face hurts." True enough, the spackling of tiny white blisters across the burned red flesh of her forehead and under her eyes was visible now. Oh, merciless sun. His too, if he'd look in the mirror. Both of them, aglow. He felt good. Right. He took his daughter's hand. "That's just love, honey," he said. "Nothing but love."

FIRST ELEGY FOR TOPSY THE ELEPHANT

Executed for murder at Coney Island, Sunday, January 4, 1903

IN PACHYDERM HEAVEN NO ONE will feed you lit cigarettes. Up there, Topsy, up there the peanut harvests are always bounteous. Plump American girls in gold lamé dust your gray girth on the hour. And even your behemoth dreams are freshly mucked. In Pachyderm, you don't have to heave and ho for your supper. Tent poles and ringmasters, be damned.

Bear with me here: Some may not remember how you balked then lumbered onto the platform. May not remember that clanking conversation between shackle and chain. Remember, how Thomas Alva Edison put his bright ideas to the test and threw the switch himself—those ten convulsive and impossibly long seconds before the big dumb hump of your body lay smoldering.

That their first impulse was to hang you is too absurd to mention here, but conception is gallows enough. All we lack are hammers and planks. I'd like to say I could've made a difference. That of the thousands gathered, eagerly pinching nickels to witness this rogue justice, I would have been the one to step forward and say *no*. But there is no reason to believe I'd be any less a coward ninety-five years ago.

This is what it boils down to. Cowardice. My prayers are predictable, Topsy. I ask only that you look down upon us with your leaky and beneficent black eye. So much has fallen since your stiff-legged topple, and there is no end in sight. Over the years, I've chiseled my teeth into consonants and vowels, the entire alphabet at my disposal, and still, most days, a piteous whimper is my wisest utterance. O Topsy, I know my place. I'll bang these pots into the wee hours, celebrating. Celebrating the tiny riots, the trivial mayhems, this flea circus of fear through which I define my life.

EINSTEIN & GÖDEL: A LOVE STORY

EINSTEIN KISSES GÖDEL

My little shubunkin—he says. My sweet, my toggle switch. What business this: mind or matter. Do you? Does it? The syllabics link our particular alembic, trunk to tail. Tick tock, tick tock. My little shubunkin, my bespectacled knish. We simply are. The you of you and the I of I; a whirligig of epic proportions. Not quite complete. I want to kiss you—I think, and inasmuch as we reach futures by displacing pasts, consider it done. My toggle switch, my scrawny feast, my Singapore Sling.

GÖDEL IN THE APPLE ORCHARD

There he goes, Gödel again. Loose. Amok, even, among the fruit, tipping buckets left and right. Muckraker of the zodiac. I love him— butterchurn and backslider; try as I might I can't stop his surefooted gallop—that giddy(up) trot from tree trunk to cider press. Gödel, flat out. Incomplete from the get-go, pawning off watch fobs and (non)sense to all. See, my Gödel, curled in the grass, linens all amiss—oh sweet, scattered sauerkraut, my nudzh, my noodling noodle. My Gödel—snagged amid the appled branches. The proof is in the pudding. Nothing is as great as the space between hearts—nothing as insignificant as the distance from sun to moon, and a thing once seen cannot be unseen. Come back, liebling; we both know—there are some words the mouth cannot make.

ALBERT IN THE KITCHEN

We have these tiffs from time to time, time itself a dubious sovereign for us both—but Gödel likes his eggs just so. If _____, then _____, he claims. Either _____, or _____. Pass the salt, I say, sick to death of all the tautologies and claptrap. Talk talk talk over jam pots and pill bottles, till my noggin throbs. Go ahead, liebchen. Hurl your proofs at this leaky contraption; few things tug with the gravity of desire. There, at the breakfast table, our robes drably matched and tied tight, the Milky Way and all its cohorts swirl in his eyes, yet I can't imagine this dog-eared earth without him. Sometimes, we simply stop and bask for a moment in the lesser miracles: breath or silence. In my dream life, my other world, it goes like this: Birdy—he says, the word taking flight from the perch of his Germanic tongue. Hurtles ear-ward. Birdy—he says, and so loving the utterance, I swoon. Birdy—he says, reaches to brush toast crumbs from my moustache—You're a mess. And that, relatively speaking, is enough.

DEAREST GÖDEL, I BID YOU ADIEU

Einstein scribbles the line three four five times. Gives up, subtraction not his strong suit. What he'd rather say: My dear Gödel, my dapper dumpling, I've found *us,* finally, in the plat book. Pinned us down, so to speak, among the lines. Crisscross and fifty years later, I'll meet the screaming piha at the Baltimore Zoo. All I really want is to hold your hand there. In the house that Jack built, monkey minds the store and the nail swings the hammer. Let's, at least, have a farewell party, musical chairs and all: the *here and now* and the *after while* swapping seats. Here's a line I stole and, owing more, give to you: *like birds through an alabaster ceiling.*

Oh Gödel, rug-tugger of the cosmos, what could be more quantum than the broomstick I'm asking you to leap? I have an idea. Let's play universe. You be God.

EINSTEIN SALLIES FORTH

Bunk. Flapdoodle. Hocus-pocus and prattle. I confess. I made it up. All that hoopla over time and space, light and matter, for you, dear Gödel, all akimbo at the blackboard. Your chalky chicken scratch and come-hither theories. How could I resist? Ask me how the cedar waxwing flies, and I answer you thus: I want it. I want the gray wing and gray wing beat, I want the trilling cry and the silence that follows. The beak and hollow bones, give. If this is greed, then by god I will be greedy. Give me the flit, the flutter, the flight itself, and the spruce bough that devours it.

Gödel, my sweet, my soupspoon, I am driving a nail I cannot name into an unslakable sky. Hunker down, now; there are no instructions save forgiveness. Look how the tiny bird tips skyward, its red-flecked wings and blue and blue.

KATYN FOREST

I AM **1939** AND COLD AIR. I want a cigarette but will make do with this shovel. This shovel feels good after stale bread and weeks in the dark. To have purpose satisfies. I am 1939 and too young to smoke. Don't be absurd. Joseph Stalin came to dinner and refused to eat the soup. I have shovel and purpose. My hands are free only because I do not resist. I don't scream through sawdust simply because I don't scream. I am the beginning of a stamp collection: ten, meticulously affixed to a small card. I'll be found in a breast pocket, yellowed and peeling. This place is called Kosygori or Goat Hill. There are rumors of orchards in the air. All I ask, really, is that someone forwards our correspondence. It is 1939 and we are tired. There is much to be done, but patience is all we can give. For now, I'm content to lie on the twenty-one thousand eight hundred fifty-six backs of my father, press my mouth to the bullet hole at the base of his skull, and hum softly until my own drum sounds.

N SCALE

"**HEY SAMMY,**" **HER MOTHER SAYS,** like it was just yesterday. Like Samantha had been home even once in the past ten, maybe eleven, years. She hadn't. Sometimes you just don't go home. For years.

"Hey Mom," she says. "Where are you?"

"Over here," her mother says. Like everywhere Samantha looks she sees anything but model trains. She doesn't. Loops and stretches of track. Trestles. Blocking windows. Crowding doorways. Cityscapes. Countrysides. Samantha can't find her mother for all the trains. Samantha sees movement in what is supposed to be the kitchen. Her mother sits, sewing, at what used to be the supper table.

"Where's Pop?"

"Oh, you know," her mother says, too busy stitching to look up. "Doing train stuff."

Train stuff was taking over the small house even twelve, maybe thirteen, years ago. Now, every surface holds a layout. Narrow shelves built around the perimeters of every room. Tables and tables of looping railroad track. Miniature mountains. Trees, rocks, and streams. Tunnels everywhere. So deft was her father's skill with perspective and staging that trains seem to appear and disappear everywhere she looked, and the cycling whir of tiny locomotive engines deafens.

"Jesus, Mom, how do you live like this?"

Samantha's mother looks up finally. Smiles. Means it. Holds up her sewing project. "For you," she says. "Just finished," she says. "Try it on."

It's a sweater-vest with an oval patch, a stretch of stitched track and the embroidered numbers 1:160. N scale.

N scale. Even years ago, her father could wax rhapsodic all the livelong day about N scale, be equally vitriolic about HO, and believe every word. Samantha knows only that it means everything is impossibly small. Samantha raises her arms, awaits the sweater.

"Hey Pop," she says, finally, after navigating the cramped hallway to find him in a room she can't remember. A room full of trains.

"Hey Sammy," he says, like it was just yesterday. Like it hadn't been a kind of forever.

"What are you up to?" she says.

"Oh, you know he says. Just chuggin' along."

His special joke.

Samantha laughs—it is the right thing to do—then convolves her way to where he hunches over a workbench. A diorama underway. Her father holds up a tweezered figure.

"Is that…" Samantha can't finish the question.

"You," he says, with subdued pride. It's true. The red hair, the striped shirt and jeans she is wearing. The very same sweater-vest, with a microscopic oval patch, her mother had just zipped her into. "There you go," he says, placing tiny Samantha gently at the front door of an impossibly small house.

"Is that…" Samantha asks.

"Our house," he says. "Start here," he says, then leads her backward along the roads and track to where the scene becomes the story.

Her story. Her whole life story, at 1:160 scale. The textile mill that shaped generations of her family before her, perfectly rendered. Dye Creek. Sabbath Rest Presbyterian Church. The cemetery where so many relatives are buried. Where Samantha was conceived. The war memorial, its big rusty tank, graffiti, and beer cans. The dentist's office, where that thing happened. Her middle school marching band parade where it was so hot she vomited.

Samantha sees herself bent over the trash can. Almost hears the terrible rendering of Michael Jackson's "Thriller." The drugstore where she got caught shoplifting sunglasses. Foxx drive-in theater where she lost her virginity, both times. The community college. First Horticulture Technologies. Then Hospitality Management. Then Human Services. Boys she dated, and didn't. Fights. Misunderstandings. Deceptions. Losses. The car. That night in the kitchen. A stretch of bare track.

Then Samantha's father leads her past a closed door. On either side, unadorned track leads into and out of holes rough-cut into the walls. It might have been her old room.

"What's this, Pop?" she asks.

Her father looks back, shrugs, smiles, means it. Smiles again.

"Come this way, Sammy," he says. Takes her hand. Leads her to the new diorama. "Here's my favorite part," he says, positioning their tiny house, with tiny Samantha at the door, her tiny mother and father visible through tiny windows. Their house sits at the end of the sceniced N scale world. Everything before it, richly detailed. Beyond, a trackless nothingness so full of potential that the air in her life-sized world practically sizzles and pops. Samantha leans in, kisses her father's cheek.

"There's a lot left to do," he says. Takes her hands in his. Samantha smiles.

"Mom," she calls out. "Mom, are you coming?"

COPY-CO.

Danny Yoder didn't know about the Komodo dragon that escaped from the Pittsburgh Zoo. Nor did he expect his bowels to seize halfway from the far side of Altoona to Moon Township, on the western edges of the 'Burgh. He blamed the scrapple and eggs. Danny Yoder didn't know they called the big lizard Noname, but was pretty sure he was getting fired when he reached Copy-Co.'s headquarters. Already late, and now the bowels.

Danny Yoder was in the middle. Of many things. The day, the week, the month. A craggy patch in his marriage. Having driven it many times, he knew there was nowhere to *go* on that empty stretch of road between Armagh and Nanty Glo. Danny Yoder liked the job. All the manuals and clear instructions. The Copy-Co. jacket with the Service Technician patch. His zip-up tool kit, impeccably organized. Liked driving his *territory*. Liked everything. Too, something unnamable about reliable duplicates comforted him.

The Porta-John took him by surprise. Danny Yoder hadn't noticed it before. Thought it must be for roadworkers. For ditch-mowers. Forsaken by PennDOT. Thought it, mostly, a godsend of sorts. Delivered on an old pallet, propped level with bricks over deeply rutted earth.

Noname, the Komodo, had slipped through a hole in the fence. Or an open gate. Nobody knew, but he had to be found. A slow killer. Patient. Three hundred pounds and ten feet long. The dragon's bite full of wicked bacteria. Its victims, if they escape those teeth, slink away to die of infection. Danny Yoder didn't know that. He also didn't know the security camera was there when he did that thing he was accused of.

Sitting in the sweltering Porta-John, Danny Yoder wondered how he got so far off track. He didn't need, didn't want, much. Hoped, one day, for the Regional Manager patch stitched to his jacket. Dreamed of raising Yorkie puppies after retiring. He'd met Jennifer at a laundromat. Milkshake stains on his Copy-Co. uniform. She sat on a washing machine, playing ukulele, singing to the wet rhythm of the heavy-duty cycle. Years ago.

Danny Yoder wasn't perfect. By now nobody expected him to be. Sometimes, he forgot Jennifer was his second. His first wife fell in with the wrong crowd. Bought a concrete goose to sit by the front steps. She dressed it for the seasons, for the holidays. A nice enough lady, but… Jennifer, the wife in the crag with him, ran twice-monthly yoga work-shops at the medium-security prison. He thought it a slippery slope. He didn't come up *that way.* He expected tarot cards to show up any day now.

The junior herpetologist was desperate. About to call his aunt, the only advertising psychic in Frostburg, Maryland. Then, there was a Noname sighting by a handful of unrelated early-morning buyers at a regular flea market way east of Pittsburgh. Hours later, Danny Yoder sat, unaware. Up and down the toilet's ribbed walls, graffiti promised, offered, cajoled. *Are You Man Enough*—the challenge, in black Sharpie, ringed the lip of the urinal funnel. Tucked behind the door's hinge spring, a handful of *Watchtower* tracts complicated the matter. *Who Controls the World? Can the Dead Really Live Again? Will Suffering Ever End?*

Danny Yoder wondered if, maybe, it *was* his fault. He remem-bered his grandmother. "Es gebt viele schwatze kieh, awwer sie gewwe all weissi millich," she'd say. *There are many black cows, but they all give white milk.* Or, "Sis alles hendich eigericht." *All is handily arranged.* His grandfather only talked about potatoes. "Ich hab en aker grummbiere geblanst." There, in the rank blue plastic confessional, lightheaded, sweaty, and shaking, guts in tumult, ashamed, worried, Danny Yoder was ripe for an epiphany. Just about to figure things out. Then Noname, the Komodo, all thump and elbows, crawled from beneath the Porta-John.

Scared Danny Yoder nearly to death. The quaking at his feet. The hellish hiss. A raking of claws. He had so much left to do. To say. When death didn't come, Danny Yoder had decisions to make. Funny how crisis can clarify things.

Danny Yoder took a deep breath. Steeled his nerve. Nudged the Porta-John door open with the toe of his serviceable work boot. Found himself eye-to-eye with the big lizard. Danny Yoder bit his lip. Noname's yellow tongue whispered secrets from its forked tips. Even before the zoo truck skidded to a stop, Danny Yoder knew everything was going to be alright. Okay. Alright.

CUTOUT

"**I HAVE SOMETHING TO TELL YOU,**" he says, coming through the back door too carefully, and because his wife doesn't seem to hear he tries again, "I have something." But not until he props the life-sized full-color, high-gloss cardboard cutout of *Olga, Russian Massage* against the churning dishwasher and in her line of sight, does he get a response.

"Oh," she says.

He knows the dishwasher is less than half full. Damn her. Way less. He goes for the jugular.

"I think I'm in love," he says.

Life-sized Olga is taller than her husband. She tries to, but can't, imagine his pale belly flesh jiggling beneath Olga's broad spread fingers. A pretty good man, though soft, and softening. Over the years, he'd been distracted. Occasionally. Last time, it was bonsai trees. Prune and snip. Then came the nightmares of being bared to the world, feet bound in a shallow pot of black earth, arms splayed; torso trunk, and limbs wrapped tight in copper wire.

There's still a withered mugo pine on the windowsill in the walk-out basement, in its tiny specimen dish, needleless and dry as bone but somehow lovely anyway. Or maybe it's on that dusty bookshelf, with his pile of blues harp instruction manuals, CDs included, and the bowl of rusting harmonicas, in the keys of A, B♭, C, D, E, F, and G. A full octave of silence.

The dishwasher kicks into rinse mode. Life-sized Olga shivers and skitters and seems about to fall. Or dance. Her husband all but lunges to the rescue.

"Have you," she begins. Doesn't finish.

Upstairs a closet door opens. Closes.

"Yes," he says and licks his fingertip to rub a smudge of road grime from life-sized Olga's shiny and bare kneecap. Until very recently, during business hours, life-sized Olga lived, stood guard, beckoned from the mouth of a narrow and crumbling parking lot of what used to be a 7-Eleven.

The wife remembers buying Slurpees there. Now, the space is shared by an outpatient clinic where she gets treatment for her varicose veins and *Olga, Russian Massage*. Olga, with her too-white teeth and too-much cleavage and the tan and the hair and that accent so very evident on her public-access cable TV spots. Thick. Nasally. Heavy. Throaty. Rough. Slavic. Sexy as hell.

Maybe both of them are right in their assumptions. Maybe they are wrong. Her husband sits down, across from her at the kitchen table. Lays his forehead against the cool Formica, still a little oily from last night's dinner. Linguine with clam sauce. His wife notices, maybe for the first time, the half-dollar-sized bald spot at the crown of his head. Almost perfectly round. Eggshell white. Nearly albinal. So translucent, she thinks she can see his skull. His actual skull.

Upstairs, a toilet flushes. The gurgle rides, within the walls, down and down. There is sunlight from somewhere. It hits them all willy-nilly, and without mercy. The glint in life-sized Olga's laminated eye is too much to bear. The wife leans in. Leans in. To kiss that spot.

GROOMER

Chet Baker, the goldendoodle, doesn't really need another haircut. His nails aren't too long. No matts or clump of burs buried in those reddish curls. Chet Baker smells like a dog. But in a good way. No obvious reasons to take him back to the groomer. Damnit.

Her husband wanted to name their first child Moog, regardless of the gender. Though unconvinced, she didn't argue. Wasn't strong enough. But the miscarriage rendered the point moot. After the second miscarriage, they got a cat. Ozzy-O. Ozzy-O brought a dead bat to the back door. The bat was beheaded, tested for rabies. Poor Ozzy-O.

They tried again. Another cat. Iggy Pop peed in the sound hole of her husband's *one-day-I'm-gonna* guitar. With the third miscarriage, her husband took up knife throwing. Axes too. In the backyard. Thwack thwack thwack against the shed. Started winning ribbons and trophies; every bullseye promised the answer. But each time he brought something shiny home, it was covered in blood.

Tupac was the last cat. Predictably, tragically, ill-conceived. The last miscarriage, too. *Let's try a new genre*, she suggested. *A different mood.* Chet Baker's appeal was deceptive. Beautiful, surely, but there was no soul behind those black eyes. The Paws-N-All groomer, on the other hand, was a truly gorgeous creature. Drop-dead so.

Anal glands! Chet Baker needs his anal glands expressed. Probably. She picks a paisley shirt with buttons. She wants a hobby. A pastime less sharp than grief. She takes her bra off, puts it back on, then off again. Dabs a little rouge between her boobs. *Not bad*, she thinks, *for thirty-three.* Thwack. Thwack. Thwack. Her husband is in Corning for the weekend. A throwing tournament. Everybody gets in free at the Museum of Glass. Winner gets an Art of Blowing class. She makes a decision. To bring the groomer home. The groomer. Syd, says the name tag. A boy-girl, or girl-boy. Hard to tell. Her heart, impounded by hurt, hurls against a paisley swirl.

Chet Baker snouts into her crotch. Wants her to hurry up. Syd has tattoos. Too many. And different-colored hair every time. And that mouth. It can't quite smile. Sallow skin, and junkie-sunk eyes, ravenous eyes. Begging to be mothered. Or fucked. Syd smells like a dog, but in a good way.

Last time, Syd made a joke about shaving around Chet Baker's balls. Or maybe it was a parable. She was too flushed—and, truth be told, wetted—to focus. The Paws-N-All loyalty card slipped between her fingers, to the floor. Syd fetched it for her. Fire.

Where is that card? One more paw stamp and she gets a free Flea & Tick Dip. She reaches for it in the folds of her purse, finds instead the tip of the guitar pick. It cuts her deep, that pick, right under the thumbnail. The quick. She cries out. And the moment cracks her rouged sternum, parts her eager ribs, fills her with memory. Their first date, before he was her husband, or anything. Him nervously saying he *played a little guitar.* By the third date he'd written a song with her name in it. Told her of his dreams of gigging at local open mics. They tried a Bob Marley song together. It was a disaster.

There is blood all over the Paws-N-All loyalty card. She puts it in the bottom of her sock drawer. There is a pounding. Or a rhythmic pulse. In her head. Out of her head. Could be her heartbeat. Could be worry or want or love. Or the ghosts of blades being sharpened. Schick schick schick. She takes off the paisley shirt, puts her bra back on. Digs through the dirty laundry for one of his Runner-Up shirts, the one with a bullseye print. Goes to the fridge. Gets an all-beef hotdog from the meat drawer. Bites it clean in half, then calls Chet Baker. "Chet Baker," she says. "Come!" Chet Baker sits at her feet, tongue out, and nothing but want in those black eyes. "Who's a good boy?" she says. "Who's a good boy?"

PAR

IN YOUR DREAM LIFE YOU ARE a midlist superhero. Look at you go, in your classic attire. The tasseled wing tips. The argyle socks. Those knickers and the jaunty flatcap. Look how you pop up all over town, in the nick of time, with your set of special clubs. The drivers and their titanium heads, the long irons, the chipper and pitching wedge, graphite shafts everyone. And, of course, the endless supply of magical balls that appear, perfectly balanced, each time you drive a tee home. Watch. See how you right the small but important wrongs. How you rain down benevolence, justice, mercy, love, even…even love, with an expertly placed ball. That scorecard you carry? Nothing less than a window into everything.

See that boy, who just needs to go up those steps and through that door.

Look there. The old woman sobbing at her old husband's sock drawer.

And that little girl, trying so hard to hold her belly in.

In the movie version of your life, anywhere can be a tee box in a pinch. You keep a tee chewed sharp in your mouth. Ready. Days off, you scrape caked mud from the clubheads. Shine your shoes. You polish everything. You scan the headlines, the classifieds, looking for leads and tips. Maybe testimonials, too.

One time, a man and a woman sat in the small meditation garden between the alley and the back door of a tired church. Sat in the shadow of a faux marble kneeling Jesus. Even you had a hard time with that one. Even you couldn't tell who'd been more crucified.

In your fantasy world, you want them all to call you Lord Mulligan, but it hasn't caught on. You'd like a small plaque, maybe hanging in the prothonotary's office at the courthouse, or near the reference desk at the library. Lord Mulligan. You like the way it lays on your tongue.

Did you see Lord Mulligan's chip shot? somebody might ask.

I was there, they could say.

I bore witness. Lord Mulligan's draw. His fade. They could say.

"Papa," she says. But it takes twice to breach your revelry. "Did you see that, Papa?"

"Yeah," you say. For realsies, because it was your turn, you drove the minivan, bursting at the welded seams with eleven-year-old girls, to Yoder's Goofy Golf. To sit on the benches shaped like donkeys or hay bales or wagon beds and keep score. A smiling dinosaur guards the eleventh hole. And at the end, a massive plaster Amish farmer looms over all. Probably Yoder himself. "Yeah," you say. Must have been a hole in one. You didn't see it. Not really.

In real life, a hot rope of doubt and inadequacy runs from your right big toe up your leg to knot at the base of your spine. No. Your sciatica is flaring. That's all. In real life, the girls are gaggled on the third hole, talking about their "oobie-bays" and laughing and laughing and laughing. Next hole over, with the tractor and plow theme, some teen boys keep singing a song about *going to Pound Town.*

"Did you see that, Papa," she says. And fear seizes your fingers. Except that it's only arthritis, and really only bad some mornings. There's fear there, sure. And doubt and worry and the rest. But that's not all. That other stuff, sneaky and sweet and delicious, is hard to grasp but it's there, and if you'll let it, it'll lift you to your feet and pull you on along. "Yeah," you say, and know the lie is one of the okay kind. Little and white. "Yeah," you say. You think you're doing a good job, good enough, but you keep checking that scorecard. Making sure the numbers add up right.

HAD A GIRLFRIEND ONCE

Had a girlfriend, once. Mistook her for a prie-dieu. Spent years kneeling on her clavicles. In prayer. Casting prayers hither and yon. Had a girlfriend once. Mistook her for a bonsai tree. Pitch pine. Or common yew. Wound her limbs tight in copper wire. Set her just so. Just so. Started to prune. All for naught. She kept insisting on her human form. Had a girlfriend. Once. Mistook her for Niagara Falls. See me up there in my stupid barrel, certain, every time, I'll survive the drop. Had a girlfriend once. Mistook her for a placeholder. Misplaced her all the livelong day. Once. I had a girlfriend. Or maybe a secret. I hid behind the mirror. She hid in my sock drawer. Nights, we'd come out, sit on the love seat, hold hands. We'd watch, only, the Weather Channel. Believing. Believing. Every word.

THE POET'S HUGE HANDS

THE POET'S HUGE HANDS SEEM beyond his control. They, the woman, the man, notice them first at the poetry reading as he reads from his book of poems. The poems were small, delicate, lush, fierce, but could not be seen for the size of his huge hands. It was hard to think about anything else. Then or later. Neither the man nor the woman stood in line for a signed copy. Afraid of what they might witness. Late winter, the poet's huge hands made a Hitchcockian cameo at Groundhog Day. Punxsutawney Phil was overshadowed for much of the rest of his life. Once, at church, they, the congregation, turned their eyes from God. Sang *He's got the whole world in his hands.* The poet and his huge hands may or may not have stormed out. Word came that he was invited to the annual Hieronymus Bosch parade in the Netherlands, where magic fills the river. When the poet said yes, the event was canceled. The poet's huge hands love the idea of tools. But only. Rumor has it that the poet and his huge hands have gone east, into exile. One hand is a war correspondent, they say. The other, deep in the trenches. Precious few appreciated the subtle and alternating asymmetry of the poet's huge hands. Now right. Now left. The man from long ago goes to the kitchen, in the wee hours. To make a sandwich. Ham and cheese maybe. He stops to wonder about his wife. Hasn't seen her since the poetry reading, so taken was she by the poet's huge hands.

THERE IS A PLAUSIBLE EXPLANATION FOR WHY THE BRILLIANT, THOUGH FURTIVE, APIARIST WAS FOUND BURIED BENEATH AN AVALANCHE OF ANTIQUE WOODEN CRUTCHES, MILDEWED CRUTCHES OF EVERY IMAGINABLE SIZE, SAID TO HAVE COME FROM THE BASEMENT OF THE ABANDONED ALTOONA ARTIFICIAL LIMB & APPLIANCE COMPANY, NOW FOUND HEAPED WILLY-NILLY ATOP SAID HONEYMONGER, ON THE DARK AND BARREN LOADING DOCK ONLY HOURS AFTER THE INAUGURAL ANNUAL SOCIETY FOR SURREALIST STUDIES CONFERENCE ENDED

But we are not at liberty to divulge any details. Suffice it to say, had the overnight custodian not slipped out to smoke—an act fully in flagrant disregard of all the rules—and heard the faint cry—*Save the little ones…save the little ones*—this report would have had a radically different conclusion.

EROTICA FOR THE
21ST CENTURY

AND THEN SHE RIPPED OFF my mask. And then I ripped off her mask. And then we put them back. Hers on my face. Mine on hers.

THE SUMMARIST

THE SUMMARIST WALKS INTO THE MEETING. Sits at the head of the table. Both lauded and feared, the Summarist. Scribbles something on a legal pad. Spins the pad into view. Walks out. My god, the lives. My god, the money. The Summarist shows up in an apartment. High above. In a kitchen. A husband skulks into the bedroom. A wife eyes, through smudged glass doors, a balcony. Don't ask the Summarist what he thinks about the library. As for the library's opinion, don't ask. The Summarist shows no mercy. See him in the Hallowed Halls. Whittling down. Encapsulating. If the Summarist could do anything else, he'd operate heavy equipment. Backhoes and bulldozers. Earthmovers, and the like. The Summarist studies the early universe. Has nothing to add or subtract. The Summarist at the café, lunching. The menu meets his approval. The Summarist, gloating, sated, distracted, steps in front of a speeding Uber. Obituary reads, simply, *Died.* Gravestone reads, simply, *Died.* The Summarist would consider the font a little froufrou. To be sure, the residents of either Heaven or Hell are quaking in their holy or hot boots.

GENDER REVEAL

NOBODY NOTICED THE FRAYED GUY-WIRE. How could they? It arced practically out of the heavens, from the tippy top of the communications tower and angled down through all kinds of sky to the concrete anchor buried deep in a weedy patch behind The Club. Back between the sand trap and a water hazard at the thirteenth hole. Invisible even from the tee box of fourteen.

Nobody was looking anyway. Not at the rusting five-gauge, one-inch diameter wire, with several of its nineteen steel strands worn through. They looked up, yes, but not at the high tower festooned with parabolic satellite dishes and chunky radio head receivers, oceans of data incessantly raging overhead, more megabits per second than one could shake a stick at. Nor did they notice the buzzards roosting up there, their whole feathered selves—the shafts and barbs and vanes—all tingly from the constant wash of data, coming and going and looking down, their black wingspans casting airplane-sized shadows.

For sure, The Club was the right choice for the party, with its tepid saltwater pool, a menu that got creative with fried things, with its view of the mountains, good Wi-Fi, a waitstaff who knew their place, and a discerning membership committee. Everybody was there. The father-to-be's hunting buddies. The expectant wife and her yoga cadre (some more lithe than others). A few folks angling for grandparent status. He loved hunting. Wanted a son but fantasized about teaching a daughter the kill shot. She, the pregnant one, had gas and heartburn. Was already stockpiling her postpartum wardrobe and making spa appointments.

Not buzzards. Not the tower. What everybody watched was the catapult dragged to the front of the deep patio, and the table of shotguns—loaded for bear—beside it. An ad hoc trebuchet, built in the beer-soaked four-car garage cum workshop of the father's best friend by mechanically minded men. It only took one boozy night to conceive of the idea—the gender reveal party surprise technology—and another to build it. Of course, they ruled out the piñata. And nixed the myriad smoke bomb options because everybody did those. No, this had to be spectacular. It had to win.

In the hung sling of the cocked catapult rested a papier-mâché sphere the size of a beach ball, with yards of gold and silver foil and multicolored streamers plastered to its surface. Inside the ersatz star, a secret to all but a few present, was a cute little live piglet with plastic angel wings, drooping off-kilter, wired around its trembling neck. He'd been in there for hours already, in the near dark, and even with the breathing holes, was too weary to squeal in distress anymore, which nobody heard over the din of the party anyway.

It was 12:25. The waitstaff just clearing lunch plates shellacked with BBQ sauces. All the men took their positions. His friends took up the shotguns. He, a throwing hatchet, and stood by the catapult. He loved hatchets. And barbeque. And hunting. At precisely 12:37—which was as accurate as the couple could be about the time of conception during an impromptu Port-a-Potty tête-à-tête after that one political rally—he'd drop the wielded blade, severing the leather thong—that she'd made without telling anyone out of the bodice worn that day—releasing the catapult, and the shiny foil star, with its cargo of faux angel piglet, would be hurled heavenward. And they'd all take aim.

Nobody knew how the cable got so frayed. Maybe it was the wind blowing over the taut steel for all those years. The harmonic-rich note of the hundred-foot guy-wire, rising and falling, the breath of Aeolus, heaving day and night. Nobody but the best friend knew how the angel piglet, first flung, then shot, blasted out of its pasted prison, would reveal baby's gender. The blue. Or the pink. How the pink? How the blue? Lord knows, expectation was thick in the air, greased all the chins, dripped from all the fork tines.

He was looking at her, she looking at him, they gawked at them, and each other. All those eyes, maws of curiosity and conniving. My god, the looks. The time, as time does, came. Bravely, the axe fell. The catapult whipped. The boys and all those blued hard barrels pointed skyward.

Nobody had considered trajectory. The secret-laden projectile hit the communications tower. The guy-wire snapped. The tower buckled, wrenching metal crying out, fell, crushed the patio and the party on it. Killed everybody but the waitstaff. It's possible that the thick swirl of 5G data kept the buzzards aloft and clacking their beaks until it was time to eat. It's a fact that the angel-winged piglet, once released, freed, put those wings to use, and aloft as well, circled the carnage, getting tips and counsel from his new feathered friends. Waiting for his moment of glory. Holding tight to his secret—because he was just a pig, he didn't understand that there was nobody left to care about the baby's gender. There, look at him go, flapping those absurdly small wings right over the mountain.

THINGS TO DO WITH DEAD ME

Before butterflies were invented, pawpaw trees still needed to be pollinated so as to grow those squishy white mango-nana-like fruits. They'd hang dead things near the trees. Flies did the sexy/dirty work. Go ahead. Hang me near the ground in a grove of pawpaws. You'll all feast soon.

Surely there's some work for me near the dumpster at the Pennsylvania Game Commission where hunters tuck the heads of killed deer to be tested for *wasting away disease.*

Or, have my funeral every Tuesday morning, for years. Each time in a different church. Talk only about my jigger collection.

Somebody suggested renting me out for dioramas. For kids' birthday parties. Crime scenes. Live Nativities. Any time a distraction is needed.

Strap me in the front car of the scariest roller coaster at Hersheypark. All but my arms. Let them flop around. Keep the brats in order.

Those life drawing classes at the community college. I can hold a pose forever.

Speaking of community college, once I saw a sign on a door, No Cadavers Today. What a magic time, I thought. Nobody dead.

My best offer? Pass my body around for the bullets of all those sad angry boys needing to shoot some body. I'll wear any kind of mask they need.

Or we could go to a movie. I like sad ones. I like funny ones. Could even be a rom-com. You pick. I'm not one of those dates who talks in the movies. I probably won't say anything at all.

NINE-BALL

WHEN I TAKE MY DROWNED BROTHER to the pool hall, we always get a table. Nobody likes to get dripped on. Not the Thursday night frat boys, with their AXE bodywash and their half-dressed girlfriends. Not the oily regulars from the train-yard shops a few blocks away. They laugh too loud, but we all know why. I'd rather play nine-ball, but my drowned brother only remembers the rules to eight-ball. Either way, I'm the one who has to balance him against the table, to wrap his stiff fingers around the cue stick and line up the shot. Every shot.

Nobody likes to get dripped on. It's hard. Work. I have to tell all the old jokes and laugh at them too. Sometimes the gravy-fries are too much to bear. Sometimes I pretend to be outraged when the waitress offers him a beer. *Can't you see he's drowned!* But on bad nights, I order him one. Drink them both when I think nobody's looking.

The Whistlestop doesn't have the best pool tables in town, but they know us. There's a high stool by the bathroom door where I can prop him when I go in for paper towels to mop up the constant puddles. One time, I needed a break. I'd scratched my shot, the cue ball ricocheting hard into a side pocket. Two girls in a booth by the pinball machine laughed. Maybe at me, maybe not. My drowned brother had that look on his face. I was pissed. I wedged him between the wall and the pinball machine. Went for a walk around the block. Outside, everything smelled of kitchen grease blown from a vent in the brick wall, of stale beer, of diesel fuel. Way up in the sky, a hook moon tore a hole in a cloud. It was beautiful in its own way. Everything.

I went back into the Whistlestop with a big heart. Found my brother in that booth with those two girls. One sitting on his lap. Maybe it was their doing. Maybe they invited him. But I know for a fact that you can never really trust the drowned. They play by their own rules. I got that girl off his lap. The backs of her thighs, damp and goosefleshed. Her shorts soaked through, and everybody could see her black panties. My brother let me win the next few games.

Most nights, it's not so high-drama. But, always, every night, just before we leave, we stuff five whole dollars in quarters into the jukebox. *What do you want to hear?* I ask. Though I know. It's our private joke. A-33. "Achy Breaky Heart." The most annoying song ever written. A-33. I punch that number. Twenty times, twenty-five cents per play. And we rush for the door. Me, more often than not, dragging my drowned brother behind. It pisses everybody off. Real bad. Every time. We laugh, real hard. Every time. I keep an eye peeled for trouble, though. But rest a little easier with my brother as an ally. I figure, he'd be pretty good, in the unlikely event of a knife fight. Him being already dead and everything.

YOU GO HOME

YOU GO HOME. EXCEPT THAT it's not home. You go to bury your father. Except that he's not dead. But you go. The drive is treacherous and tedious, then tedious and treacherous. Raw mountains claw at gray skies. The road is clotted with trucks. A churning asphalt river. Leafless, the forests. The esophagus. There may have been an ice storm. There should have been. An ice storm. You might be by yourself. You can't tell. You go home. Except. And at the supper table everyone eats their bowls of shattered glass. Every time. You can't tell teeth from shard these days.

You go home. Again. On a motorcycle, sometimes. Sometimes on a banjo. Except that it's not home. These days. Again. Alone or not. Again. You go to bury your father. Talk of plots. Or not. Especially not. Except that he's not dead. Still. Calls you by other names. Names others. Asks if it's raining. If it's going to rain. Asks if it's raining. If it's going to rain. Asks if it's raining. If it's going to rain. Now it's the supper table. Now not. Give us this day. Later you find your mother. She stands at his dresser, the sock drawer open. She cries softly. Not talking. It's always the sock drawer. Open.

Again. You go home. Leave the house because you've been leaving the house since forever. The scuppernong wine isn't enough to keep you. Home. The bar by the lake is not home. Festooned with fishnets and anchors and implacable longing. Christmas stockings. The bar is called Lintheads. You go there. Small talk. All talk. Any talk, really, but talk of your dead father. Keep talking, you say and can't stop looking at her green-and-red socks. She tells you a story. The lake is man-made. The water is not. But there's a town under the water. A whole town. Drowned. They dammed the river. The river swallowed an entire cotton mill, the stores, row after row of crackerbox houses. Ah, Lintheads, you think, or say aloud. Or maybe you mentioned your dead father, not dead. These days you can't tell shard from truth. Keep talking, you say but she must've slipped out while you were not. Talking.

You wonder if all the people who've drowned in the lake over the years and will drown in the lake in years to come, go to live in the drowned town. Work in the drowned cotton mill. Dwell in the drowned mill houses. Eat drowned cornbread and drowned beans. And all that drowned talk. Or not. These days. In the parking lot you hear the looms clacking madly away deep beneath the water's still, dark surface. In the parking lot the gibbous moon spits in your eye. Eyes you. Close them, those eyes, and you hear the footsteps of all the dead shuffling along the lake bed, going about their dead business. Keep talking, you say.

Not drowning. Not yet. Drowning. You go back. Home. Back. Home. Except. In case your father is there one last time.

ACKNOWLEDGMENTS

These works were previously published.

"My Brother, Named & Unnamed." *Fractured* Literary. Monsters, Mystery, & Mayhem Prize. November 2021.

"Let's Say, Triptych." *CRAFT* Literary. Flash Fiction Contest. September 2020.

"Altar Call." *New Micro*. Norton Press. 2018.

"Which Story?" *Sudden Stories*. Mammoth Books. 2003

"Katyn Forest." *Best American Poetry 1997*.

"Which Story?" *Another Chicago Magazine*. 1995.

STEVEN SHERRILL is not, absolutely not, a traditional academic, nor a scholar. But Steven Sherrill has been making trouble with words since eighth grade, when he was suspended from school for two weeks for a story he wrote. He dropped out of school in the tenth grade, ricocheted around the southern United States for years, eventually earning a welding diploma from a community college, which led circuitously to an MFA in poetry from the Iowa Writers' Workshop, and as of recently, professor emeritus of English and integrative arts at Penn State University, with five novels, a book of poems, and a memoir in the world.

His first novel, *The Minotaur Takes a Cigarette Break*, is translated into eight languages and was released as an audio book. His second novel, *Visits from the Drowned Girl*, published by Random House (and nominated by them for the Pulitzer Prize) in the United States and Canongate, United Kingdom, was released in June of 2004. *The Locktender's House*, novel number three, was released by Random House in Spring 2008. In November 2010, CW Books released the poetry collection, *Ersatz Anatomy*. Louisiana State University Press: Yellow Shoe Fiction Series released the novel *JOY, PA*, in March 2015. *The Minotaur Takes His Own Sweet Time* was published in the fall of 2016 and lauded by Alan Gurganus in *The New York Times Book Review*. *Motorcycles, Minotaurs, &* *Banjos*, the memoir, is a book about twenty-one days and sixty years. A motorcycle ride down the spine of Appalachia, with a little banjo and big myth for company, to play and sing at the graves of dead banjo heroes. It's about making a life *about* making work.

www.ingramcontent.com/pod-product-compliance
Lightning Source LLC
Chambersburg PA
CBHW070253310726

48976CB00008B/2638